Accommodations

A Comedy in Three Acts

by Nick Hall

A SAMUEL FRENCH ACTING EDITION

SAMUEL FRENCH

FOUNDED 1830

New York Hollywood London Toronto

SAMUELFRENCH.COM

ACCOMMODATIONS was originally produced in dinner theatre by Josh Cockey, with direction by James Peacock, setting by Jay Scott and lighting by Judy Hashagen, at the Limestone Valley Dinner Theatre, Cockeysville, Maryland on October 31st, 1973 with the following cast:

CAST
(*In Order of Appearance*)

TRACY	*John Bartholomew*
LEE	*Hollice Stander*
PAT	*Nancy Linehan*
BOB	*Jon Barry Wilder*

CHARACTERS

TRACY

LEE

PAT

BOB

SETTING

An apartment near Sheridan Square, New York City.

ACT ONE

Friday afternoon

ACT TWO

SCENE 1: Saturday afternoon, a week later

SCENE 2: Later the same night

ACT THREE

Sunday morning

Accommodations

ACT ONE

The setting is the larger of the two rooms that comprise the apartment. There is a front door and the doorway to the bedroom. One corner of the room is the kitchen. It contains an old refrigerator, an old stove and, under the hinged kitchen counter top, an old bathtub. There is no sink. The kitchen is not in any way partitioned off or separated from the rest of the room. The room is unattractively furnished with odd pieces of furniture collected from the streets. There is a large ottoman that converts into a bed. There is no couch or sofa. There may be a couple of kooky touches, but nothing extreme. The bedroom doorway has a curtain and over that a bead curtain. The apartment is not attractive.

At rise the stage is empty. A phone, not visible, is ringing. At the same time we hear the front door being unlocked, it opens and TRACY *enters. He is an attractive young student, wearing a coat and tie and carrying a suitcase and an overnight bag. He closes the door and registers the phone ringing.*

TRACY. Anyone home? (*Still carrying his luggage he moves round the room looking for the phone. His search leads him offstage into the bedroom. After a moment he re-enters without his luggage. He is following, hand over hand, the trail of the telephone cord. The trail leads him round several pieces of furniture to the kitchen, where, amazed, he discovers the phone in the bathtub. He picks up the receiver.*) Hello . . . No, this is Tracy . . .

5

Tracy Varetta . . . I'm the new roommate . . . No,
Pat isn't here. Nobody's here but me . . . I just moved
in . . . Just now . . . Yes, I'm a student . . . Psychology N.Y.U. . . . Well, right now I'm studying the
effects of pollution and poor air quality on the lives of
overcrowded rats . . . Whaddya mean I moved into the
right place? . . . Yeh, I'll tell Pat you called . . . Okay,
I'll tell him. (*Hangs up. He puts the phone back into the
tub, realizes what he's doing and puts it on a table. He
exits to the bedroom and re-enters almost immediately
carrying a towel and a shaving kit. He is taking off his
jacket as he enters. He starts undressing, and has probably got his tie off, his shoes off, and his shirt unbuttoned
when the phone rings again. He picks up the phone.*)
Hello, Pat's out and so is Lee . . . Oh, Brian, I just got
here. (*Dry.*) I want to thank you for recommending the
roommate agency . . . The apartment? (*Looking
around.*) It's . . . It's . . . It's cheap. Two rooms . . .
No, not two rooms and a bathroom—two rooms . . . I
haven't met them yet. Three of us. Pat's been living here
and Lee and I are moving in today. Listen, I want to
take a bath so if you . . . What? . . . Yeah, I got most
of my stuff. Nearly everything but the T.V. and one suitcase . . . Right now? I was going to come over this
evening . . . You had to pick today to leave town . . .
(*Starts re-dressing.*) Twenty minutes! . . . You're crazy.
It's not possible . . . Okay, I'll take a cab . . . Yes, the
rats are fine, thank you . . . No, Jackson is no longer
with us . . . His mother ate him . . . Why had I better
be careful? . . . I know we're going to be overcrowded,
but I'm living with two fellahs not my mother. Will you
get off the phone. Bye (*Hangs up.* TRACY *has got his
coat and tie back on. He tosses his towel and shaving kit
off into the bedroom. He starts to put on his shoes. He
has got one of them on when there is a knocking at the
front door. With an exclamation of exasperation, he gets
second shoe partly on and hobbles to the front door. He
opens it.* LEE SCHALLERT, *an attractive woman in her*

thirties, is outside. TRACY *does not pause, but pushes past*
LEE.) Everybody's out. (*Exits.* LEE *looks after him for
a moment, puzzled, then enters the apartment. She
carries in addition to her handbag a large open carry-all.
She is obviously horrified by the apartment. The front
door is still open.* LEE *takes a skillet and a small clock
out of her carry-all. She puts the skillet on the stove and
finds somewhere to put the clock. From off-stage we hear*
PAT *call.*)

PAT. See ya in a minute, Simon. (LEE *sees a roach and
jumps back startled. She grabs a newspaper or something
and chases it, striking at it. It apparently scurries to the
front door. Just as* LEE *on hands and knees, raises the
paper to hit it on the doorsill,* PAT *appears in the doorway and stamps on it.* PAT *is a young girl in her early
twenties, dressed at the moment as Shirley Temple, including hair and make up. She carries a very large lollipop, and a small grocery sack, which she soon puts
down.*) Hi! I'm Pat. (*Pause.* LEE *is stunned.*) You must
be one of the new roommates. Lee or Tracy. What are
you staring . . . (*Realizes.*) Oh, gosh, I'm sorry. It's my
costume for a show I'm in. Well, curtains up on your
new home. Three single girls in an apartment in New
York. Do you love it?

LEE. No, I hate it.

PAT. From this very window we have an almost un-
obstructed view of seven fire escapes.

LEE. They said it was furnished.

PAT. It is. (*Points.*) The bedroom's through there.
(LEE *looks.*)

LEE. There are three of us.

PAT. The bed sleeps two and (*Gesturing to the ottoman.*) that's convertible.

LEE. Where's the bathroom?

PAT. Well, over here we have this really ingenious idea.
It's a clever little combination sink and bathtub.

LEE. You mean there's a bathtub in the kitchen and
no sink anywhere?

PAT. It sounds nicer when I say it.

LEE. Where's the rest of the bathroom?

PAT. (*Pointing off through the front door.*) Out there.

LEE. Would you repeat that. I think I'm going deaf.

PAT. Out there. The next door on the left down the hall.

LEE. It's hard to believe I gave up a split-level in Westchester for this.

PAT. You'll love it.

LEE. I love Central Park, but I wouldn't want to sleep in it.

PAT. We'll fix it up. I'm Pat Murray.

LEE. Lee Schallert. (*Shake.*) I really didn't know what to expect.

PAT. I know, the roommate agency didn't give much information. They said Tracy was a student, but nothing about you.

LEE. And somehow I thought the apartment was going to be . . .

PAT. Better?

LEE. (*Quickly.*) Bigger. I thought they meant two room *and* a bathroom.

PAT. It'll work out. Three single girls in an apartment. What do we need? Somewhere to sleep and a place to wash stockings. I'm an actress—almost . . . I study and audition and work part time when I have to.

LEE. How long have you been here?

PAT. Three months.

LEE. Did you have roommates before? Before Tracy and me?

PAT. Nine.

LEE. Nine!

PAT. Not all at once. It wasn't so bad; five of them actually paid their share of the rent. But finally the fast turnover was making me dizzy. So I decided I'd get more stable roommates through an agency. At least the agency checks people out. You know they're going to be who they say they are.

LEE. I lied to the agency. (*Pause.*)

PAT. What about?

LEE. I said that I was single. Well, I am single. I'm single with a husband.

PAT. How does that work?

LEE. I left my husband.

PAT. When?

LEE. This morning. I mean I'd decided to before, but actually this morning.

PAT. Does he know where you are?

LEE. No. I didn't leave an address or phone number. Only Miriam, my best friend, knows I'm here.

PAT. What's he like?

LEE. Bob—he's very nice. Warm, intelligent, handsome, amusing.

PAT. Those are great reasons to leave him.

LEE. It's hard to explain.

PAT. Do you love him?

LEE. (*Pause.*) I don't know.

PAT. (*Brightly, changing subject.*) Don't know! When I fall in love everybody knows. It's always a huge wither-thou-goest-grow-old-along-with-me-count-the-ways   passion. The earth stands still and it's forever. I did that three times last week.

LEE. What happened?

PAT. They fell in love with me too, which takes all the fun out of it. Anyway I've got a career to think about.

LEE. Say, as I came in a guy was leaving here. Who was that?

PAT. Could've been anyone. Several friends have keys.

LEE. Well, I'm glad I'm here. (*Looks around.*) Not ecstatic, but fairly glad—

PAT. You didn't bring much luggage.

LEE. It's coming. There's a fellah bringing it over.

PAT. What do you do?

LEE. I'm a substitute teacher.

PAT. You should work part time in a drugstore like me. Talent scouts almost never discover substitute teachers.

LEE. I haven't any talent, and I don't want to be discovered. I'm a person not a South Sea Island.

PAT. Look on the bright side. The worse the situation, the funnier it is. Know what I mean?

LEE. Like if I take a long hard look at this apartment, I'll become hysterical. Sure. I'll buy that.

PAT. That's not what I meant. It's just an attitude. Maybe it comes with the costume.

LEE. It's a beautiful costume.

PAT. I got it from the landlord.

LEE. He rents costumes?

PAT. No, he wears them.

LEE. The landlord wears that?

PAT. Not at the moment. He's in his Dorothy Lamour period now.

LEE. What's that mean?

PAT. I dunno. Sarongs and native boys, I guess. He's got closets full of the greatest outfits.

LEE. It's a good thing I don't have any great outfits. There isn't a closet in this place.

PAT. Well, Simon's costumes—Simon is the landlord—his costumes are really useful for getting the feel of a part. And it's so convenient, his apartment is right next to ours—which reminds me, I promised to go over and help him sort things. He's gonna give me some stuff he doesn't want anymore.

LEE. I can't wait to meet Tracy. Whatever she is.

PAT. Are you used to roommates?

LEE. I'm not used to them filling the kettle from my bathtub while I'm in it.

PAT. Well, just hope we don't get a creep. We can put up with anything but a creep. And this building has its share. Simon was telling me there's this pale thin guy on the top floor. Very tall, always wears black, head to toe solid black, including, a black opera cloak. He never goes out in the daytime, and nobody sees him for weeks at a time.

LEE. Maybe he works nights.

PAT. Or changes into something. I wonder why he chose this building?

LEE. Probably reminds him of a. cemetery back home.

PAT. "La via del tren subterraneo es peligrosso."

LEE. What's that mean?

PAT. Do you speak Spanish?

LEE. No.

PAT. It means "Beware the dark that moves in the dark." (*The buzzer sounds.*)

LEE. (*Startled.*) What's that?

PAT. The front door. You have to press the button up here. It may be Tracy.

LEE. Or my luggage.

PAT. Here's the button. (*Presses it.*) Listen, I won't be long. I'm going right next door to Simon's. (*Exits leaving the door open.* LEE *unpacks a couple more everyday things from her carry-all and puts them in appropriate places. She takes out a tape measure of some sort, extends it as if to measure windows, decides not to and lays it down. She unpacks a large toy stuffed pig and puts it somewhere. She starts unpacking* PAT'S *grocery bag into cupboards and the refrigerator.*)

BOB. (*Calling from off-stage.*) Hello? Lee? (LEE *obviously recognizes the voice and does not want to meet the owner. She looks around, then crosses to the window, but cannot get it open.* BOB SCHALLERT *enters. He is a nice, bright guy about the same age as* LEE.) There you are.

LEE. (*Mock casual.*) Oh, hi, Bob.

BOB. What the hell are you doing here?

LEE. I'm living here.

BOB. Since when?

LEE. Since about ten minutes ago. How did you know where to find me?

BOB. Miriam told me.

LEE. How did you get it out of her?

BOB. Five martinis.

LEE. Why have you come bursting in here?

BOB. I didn't come bursting in. I rang every bell in the lobby and then groped my way up in the darkness.

LEE. Is the hall light out?

BOB. No, all fifteen watts are still blazing away three floors down.

LEE. You've got a lot of nerve. This is my home.

BOB. Well, since I'm your husband that makes it mine too. Tell me, what do I pay for this dump?

LEE. Not one penny. And it's not a dump.

BOB. Let me think. I got up, had breakfast, and went to work as usual.

LEE. Bob, I left you.

BOB. I came home from work early, found a note saying there was meat loaf in the refrigerator, and please water the plants.

LEE. I left you.

BOB. Drove all the way back to town, saw Miriam and found you'd left me what do you mean, you left me?

LEE. I told you this morning at breakfast.

BOB. No, you didn't.

LEE. Yes, I did.

BOB. What did you say?

LEE. I said "we can't go on like this, Bob. I'm leaving you."

BOB. (*After a tiny pause.*) And what did I say?

LEE. You said, "I can't believe the Giants are going to New Jersey."

BOB. Well, you know how I am in the morning.

LEE. I know how you are all the time; that's why I left.

BOB. Have a heart. It was seven-thirty in the morning. I had ten minutes to get out of the house. Now what's going on?

LEE. I'd rather not talk about it.

BOB. Not talk about it! You have to talk about it. (*Pause.*) Okay, we won't talk about it. But will you tell me, if I guess. (*Long pause.*) Don't look so glum. It's not the end of the world. It's apparently the end of our world but not the end of *the* world. Say something cheerful.

LEE. Nice weather we're having.

BOB. (*Glancing out of the window.*) How can you possibly tell? All you can see out of here is every fire escape in Greenwich Village. There must be hundreds.

LEE. Seven.

BOB. (*Incredulous.*) Is that all? What does this place cost?

LEE. A hundred and thirty-five.

BOB. What does that include?

LEE. Exactly what you see plus the right to privacy. The right to be an adult individual and to come and go as I please.

BOB. (*Looking around.*) If I were you, I'd go.

LEE. I wish you would.

BOB. You can't afford a hundred and thirty-five.

LEE. I've got roommates.

BOB. Roommates! For heaven's sakes, you're a married woman.

LEE. We all make mistakes.

BOB. Yeah, well, we don't all make them this big at seven-thirty in the morning.

LEE. You don't understand.

BOB. Give me time. I'm trying. At breakfast this morning you suddenly decided to leave me and the eight rooms in Westchester and move into one and three quarter rooms in Greenwich Village with a bunch of roommates so that you could have some privacy.

LEE. Two roommates. Me and two others.

BOB. Only three people in a nice roomy place like this. You probably won't see each other for days at a time.

LEE. It's very easy to be flippant.

BOB. Oh, no, it's not. The mood I'm in now, murder is easy; flippant is very, very hard. Where's the bathroom?

LEE. Which part of it?

BOB. You didn't say that.

LEE. This is part of it.

BOB. Terrific. Where's the rest of the bathroom?

LEE. Out there.

BOB. That's a great decorating idea. Really Americana. My grandmother used to have one "out there." Of course, she didn't live in Manhattan, in an apartment. Are you out of your mind?

LEE. No, I'm not. I'm saner than I've been in a long time and much happier.

BOB. You should have told me what made you happy. Everytime you felt depressed, I could've thrown a little dirt on the floor.

LEE. Along with your socks.

BOB. Leave my socks out of this.

LEE. I have. I've left your socks completely out of it along with your shirts, underwear, slacks, and that silly suede hat with the drooping canary feather.

BOB. It's a pheasant feather.

LEE. I don't care if it's a Dodo feather.

BOB. Dodos are extinct.

LEE. No wonder it droops. Or maybe it's just tired of being paired with that wilted college sweatshirt you wear as a security blanket. Why don't you get some new clothes?

BOB. I'm sorry, Bloomingdales. I must have a wrong number; I thought I was talking to my wife.

LEE. Don't call me that.

BOB. What?

LEE. Your wife. I'm a person with a name, an individual, not one of your possessions like your house, your car, your office.

BOB. You forgot something. My income which pays for your house, your clothes, your food, and your adenoidal mother's long distance phone calls.

LEE. That's going to change.

BOB. You mean she's having her adenoids out? What hospital? I'll send her something: fruit, flowers, last month's phone bill.

LEE. I'm going to live here, work, and pay my own way.

BOB. And what am I supposed to do?

LEE. You're a big boy now. Do something useful. Take up basket weaving.

BOB. Why? I'm not handicapped.

LEE. You don't have to be handicapped to weave baskets.

BOB. No, but I bet it helps. (*Irritated.*) What the hell's going on?

LEE. (*Snapping.*) You are not listening to me.

BOB. Hold it. Let's go back to last night when everything was fairly normal. You warmed up that tuna noodle thing for the third straight day, then we sat around watching T.V.

LEE. Wrong. You sat around watching T.V. I washed the dishes, cleaned the kitchen, and ironed your shirts.

BOB. Well, okay. Then you watched T.V.

LEE. No, I didn't. By that time the Giants were playing ball. So you continued watching T.V. and I wrote a letter to your mother. Did you ever think there might be something on that I wanted to watch? I'm a person too, you know.

BOB. I've never considered you anything else . . . until today. You've been great. The perfect wife.

LEE. And what am I now?

BOB. (*It is not a compliment.*) A woman.

LEE. (*Defiantly.*) I am a woman.

BOB. It's nothing to be proud of.

LEE. What d'you mean?

BOB. It's not your fault. Some people are born stupid or unhealthy, and some are born women.

LEE. You are a sexist!

BOB. I'm as normal as the next guy.

LEE. There's not going to be a next guy. I am an independent person, paying my own way, and living here alone.

BOB. What about your roommates?

LEE. I've only met one of them. Pat . . . something or other; I've forgotten.

BOB. What's she like?

LEE. Very nice. I only saw her for a moment, just before you came in.

BOB. Well, how old is she?

LEE. Twenty going on seven and a half.

BOB. What's she look like?

LEE. Shirley Temple. (*There is a very, very long pause.*) Well, aren't you going to say anything?

BOB. What can I say. I find you living in a place that God forgot with a very nice retard who looks like Shirley Temple. Who's the third roommate, Dracula?

LEE. No, he lives upstairs.

BOB. . . . One of us is crazy and I think it's you.

LEE. Well, he's not really Dracula . . .

BOB. That's a load off my mind.

LEE . . . He's just this creepy person. Very tall and thin, who's dressed completely in black and hardly ever goes out, and never during the daytime. I mean, that's weird.

BOB. Sure it is. You and Shirley Temple are just humdrum, but that's weird.

LEE. (*Irritated.*) Well, he might be dangerous. What would I do if I met him on the stairs?

BOB. Get some garlic salt and sprinkle him to death! Who else live here?

LEE. Tracy Varetta. I haven't met her yet.

BOB. Probably a hooker with poodles. (*Sees the pig, pointing.*) What's this doing here?

LEE. That's Bernice.

BOB. I know it's Bernice. What's she doing here?

LEE. She's here because when I finally looked around this morning, the only thing that I really wanted, that had anything to do with me, was Bernice.

BOB. Poor old Bernice, always snatched up at the last moment. If we'd got married in a normal place at a normal time you'd never have got her.

LEE. I had to have a bouquet and there were no flowers to be found at that time of night. I mean, you can't just stand there wearing yards of satin and lace with your arms dangling like a quarterback.

BOB. You weren't wearing yards of satin and lace.

LEE. The bride looked radiant in a rumpled blue linen suit carrying a bright yellow pig. I've always been glad that flower shop was shut.

BOB. Yeah, if it'd been open, you'd be sitting here with the oldest Lily of the Valley in the world.

LEE. And "Oklahoma" remember?

BOB. You were the one who wanted music, and that was all she could play.

LEE. Yes, but I thought she'd at least play it on the piano. There was a piano right there. Well, it was amusing.

BOB. Do you want a divorce?

LEE. I . . . I don't know yet.

BOB. As long as I live I'll never forget that night. The world's worst honeymoon.

LEE. Oh, come on, it was a lot of laughs.

BOB. You're so insensitive.

LEE. How can you say that? I wasn't the one who got drunk afterwards and ran about nude in the rain singing "Oklahoma."

BOB. I don't know "Oklahoma."

LEE. You had to know it. That dreary woman played it twenty times.

BOB. You don't play words on a trombone. The only song I have ever known how to sing is "The Holy City."

LEE. That's not what you were singing. There was nothing holy about it.

BOB. Well, anyway, we made up the next night, didn't we? (*He begins closing in on her.*) I consider that second night the real start of our marriage.

LEE. So do I. A sumptuous meal, too much wine, a long

hot bath, soft music, dim lights, and you, sound asleep already.

BOB. I was tired.

LEE. You shouldn't have run around singing the night before. You didn't move till the next morning.

BOB. But we didn't get up till three in the afternoon. Those are the best times—mornings when neither of us has to get up.

LEE. Sunday was our best day.

BOB. Especially when you remember to go by the bakery on Saturday.

LEE. And you get the Sunday paper off the lawn early.

BOB. (*Putting his arms around her.*) I think I like you best on Sunday mornings.

LEE. (*They are very intimate.*) I thought you liked the sports section best.

BOB. No, you best. I only read while you do the crossword.

LEE. I never finish the crossword.

BOB. Heaven is a Sunday morning in bed with you, the New York Sunday Times, and some crumbs from a danish pastry. This Sunday, I want a blueberry cheese danish, okay?

LEE. Okay.

BOB. What are you gonna have? (*He nuzzles her.*)

LEE. I'm not.

BOB. You're not dieting again? You don't need to. You look great.

LEE. I won't be there.

BOB. Why not?

LEE. Because I'm living here.

BOB. (*Breaking away, angry.*) What about the Merkels?

LEE. The Whats?

BOB. Merkels. Joe and Ethel Merkel and their three little Merkels. They're the nice family who employ me and they're coming to brunch on Saturday so what do I tell him?

LEE. Tell him to pick up your socks.

BOB. Look, Joe said he wanted to meet the little woman.

LEE. What little woman?

BOB. You. He wants to meet you.

LEE. Tell him you don't have a little woman. And if he's funny for dwarfs, let him find his own.

BOB. Lee, listen to me. This is very important. My boss is coming to lunch on Saturday and I can only cook bacon and eggs. What do I do?

LEE. Set the clocks back.

BOB. What do you want from me. Clothes? A new car? Money? Is that it? I'll get a raise. It's easy. All I have to do is ask Mr. Merkel on Saturday providing you're there to cook lunch and be hostess and give Mrs. Merkel some clippings from the shrubs and pretend the three little Merkels are human for God's sake, will you please come home on Saturday?

LEE. No.

BOB. Why not?

LEE. Because if I come home, I'm coming home because you want me there. Not a cook, not a maid, not a hostess and not, God forbid, a little woman, but me. That's why I left! That's why I'm staying here; and that's why I am not going to see you for six weeks.

BOB. What?!? Do you know what our kitchen's going to look like at the end of six weeks?

LEE. We are each going to spend the next six weeks as independent, adult people. I consider myself a free agent.

BOB. I know what you're saying. You're saying . . . what are you saying?

LEE. I'm saying I'm going to do what I please, when I please, where I please, with whomever I please.

BOB. You're saying you're going to fool around. That's what you're saying.

LEE. Whatever.

BOB. Never mind whatever. I want to meet whomever.

LEE. Well, you don't expect me to sit here darning and baking, do you?

BOB. Of course not. You never darned or baked when you had a home and husband; why should you start now that you're doing whatever with whomever.

LEE. I intend to do a lot of things I've never done. Sit in sidewalk cafes, go to concerts and galleries and the zoo.

BOB. Well, it's a step up from here.

LEE. And I intend to do the Sunday crossword by myself.

BOB. What's the matter with whomever? Can't he spell?

LEE. You are a male chauvinist . . .

BOB. Is that so? Well, let me tell you something from the male chauvinist point of view; I don't intend to darn and bake either, so there! I intend to have a good time, a very good time. I intend to go to the ball games and enjoy them. I intend to scream and shout with the rest of the fans secure in the knowledge that all of us together cannot equal the eternal female rustle and clatter and noise of a woman who wants attention, and they all want attention all the time. Well, you're not going to get it, not from me. You can stay here in God's Little Acre till Hell freezes over. I don't *want* to get in. But. If I did want to get in—I don't—but if I did, just remember that a wife's slum is her husband's castle. I am now going to find some whomever to whatever with. And you can tell Shirley Temple from me that when the good ship Lollipop went down, this is where the rats came. (*He crosses to the door.*)

LEE. (*A primal scream.*) That is not the last word. We do not want attention all the time. We want reasonable equality as human beings. Personally I would consider it a vast improvement if I rated as high as your Pontiac. And as for the noise, some night you should stay awake and listen to yourself snore. You can only relate to me as a stereotype you call wife. The thought of me as a person scares you to death. You don't know if I want to come back, and, what's worse, you don't even know if *you* want me to come back. You don't give one damn about me. You don't care that the bathtub's in the kitchen and the commode's halfway to Brooklyn. Or that there's a creepy psychotic upstairs with a Dracula complex. You don't care if I wake up in the middle of the night and find him slobbering over my neck.

BOB. Don't worry about it.

LEE. Why?

BOB. He's just a vampire. He's not a dumb vampire. (*Exits slamming door. LEE rushes after him and yanks the door open. She shouts after him.*)

LEE. You . . . ! I hope bacon and eggs are against the Merkel's religion. (*She crosses back into the room, leaving the door open, simply seething. She notices her wedding ring and tries to pull it off. It won't come off. She struggles with it. She goes to the kitchen and tries soap; but that doesn't work either. In a cold blooded rage she fishes in her handbag and produces a nail file, and starts filing. PAT enters from the bedroom. She is dressed as a Civil War Southern Belle. Huge crinoline skirt, sun bonnet, the whole "Gone With The Wind" bit. The costume should be a masterpiece. No old window drapes here. She strikes an elaborate pose in the bedroom door. LEE does not notice her and continues filing. Irked, PAT crosses in to just behind LEE's shoulder and strikes an even more elaborate pose.*)

PAT. (*In a very strong southern accent.*) Do you think ah dare go to Colonel Sanders' in this tacky old rag?

LEE. (*Startled, jumping.*) What? Where did you come from?

PAT. From Simon's, of course. He was "at home" this evening.

LEE. I didn't see you come in.

PAT. Well, there is a small wrought iron balcony which connects Simon's living room with our bedroom window.

LEE. Is that Simon's dress?

PAT. I think you have quite the wrong idea about Simon. He's never worn this dress. It's not his color. It's a present from a friend of his, named Rocky, who wore it in the semi-finals of the Miss America Contest.

LEE. Simon's friend Rocky was in the Miss America Contest?

PAT. That's what I said.

LEE. What was his talent?

PAT. Being there. Lee, honey, what are you doing with that emory board?

LEE. I'm taking off my wedding ring.

PAT. (*Normal voice.*) Why?

LEE. Bob was just here.

PAT. Why didn't you call me. (*Southern.*) I love to flirt with married men.

LEE. Sorry, but we like to scream in private. (*Throws nail file back in her bag.*) I wish I knew what I was going to do.

PAT. (*Cheering her up.*) Well, ah know. You put on your shawl and bonnet and we'll drive into Savannah.

LEE. (*Wan smile.*) Think we'll get there before Sherman?

PAT. Well, of course we will. There's this big effort to raise money to buy Sherman off. And they want all the young girls there in case they can't raise enough money. You know what saved Augusta, Ga., don't you?

LEE. Oh, come on. You know that story of the young girl sacrificing her virtue to save her town is a myth.

PAT. Hush your mouth! Ah myself have saved twenty-seven cities and a covered bridge.

LEE. A covered bridge?

PAT. He was only a corporal.

LEE. Don't you feel . . . well, squandered?

PAT. Lord no. I got to travel around and meet all those famous people like General Grant, and McClellan, and Sherman and Steve McQueen.

LEE. Steve McQueen wasn't in the Civil War.

PAT. (*Indignant.*) You mean that Yankee done lied to me?

LEE. They all do. Never make any kind of contract with a man; you'll find their end doesn't hold up too well.

PAT. Ma mother used to say, the only two things a gentleman has to hold well are his liquor and his women.

LEE. Bob gets drunk on three beers and I'm his women. Or was. Or were.

PAT. What tense is that?

LEE. A hypothetical subjunctive. Who cares?

PAT. You do.

LEE. No, I did. Past tense. (*Deep breath.*) So. Why don't we fix this place up?

PAT. Good idea. We could ship in lots of Spanish Moss and do the whole place Southern.

LEE. (*Takes the tape measure and pulls a chair to the window.*) Why don't we start with something simpler: like curtains.

PAT. Oh, okay. What color?

LEE. Whatever color's on sale at the stores this week. Look in my bag and see if there's paper and pencil. I wish I had my sewing machine here.

PAT. Big bag or pocketbook?

LEE. Pocketbook. (PAT *puts paper and pencil on table.*) Are you sure there are only seven fire escapes?

PAT. Yeah, I counted. (TRACY *appears in the open doorway. He carries one large suitcase and a small T.V. set.*)

TRACY. Hi, there. Where shall I put this?

PAT. Lee, where do you want the suitcases and stuff?

LEE. (*Who is busy measuring and does not see* TRACY.) In the bedroom.

PAT. (*Pointing. Very Blanche DuBois.*) Just put them in there, please, young man.

TRACY. Okay. (*Crosses to bedroom door, turns back. Slight pause.*) Listen, I was going to . . .

PAT. (*Who is taking down measurements from* LEE. *Very southern lady.*) Just put them down anywhere in there and do what you have to. (TRACY *waits one moment, shrugs, and exits to bedroom.* PAT *continues without pause.*) We could turn the place into a real mantrap. You know, soft lights, soft music and red-flocked wallpaper.

LEE. Why?

PAT. We are three defenseless girls. And ah was taught that a defenseless girl should get herself a man.

LEE. Bull. I'm not frail and I'm not defenseless, and I'm not a girl.

PAT. (*Horrified.*) You're not?

LEE. I'm a person. And if you need anything more specific than that, I'm a woman. I stopped being a girl on my eighteenth birthday. I'm an adult and I want to be treated as an adult. I'm tired of the whole male bias of our culture. It starts at birth. Rub-a-dub-dub, three men in a tub. Why three *men?*

PAT. There was an old woman who lived in a shoe.

LEE. Yes, and she had so many children she had to go on welfare. Well, this apartment is not going to be a mantrap. The sexes are equal and in this house there will be no role playing, no-boy-meets-girl, no soft-lights-soft-music-red-flocked-wallpaper.

PAT. And no fun.

LEE. There will be no sexual discrimination here. (TRACY *enters from bedroom wearing only a towel around his waist and carrying a toilet kit. He crosses in front of* LEE *and* PAT *to the bathtub and starts taking out his shaving things.*)

PAT. Si el tren se para entre la estaciones quedesa adentro!!!

LEE. What's that mean?

PAT. Wow!!

LEE. (*To* TRACY.) What do you think you're doing?

TRACY. I'm gonna take a bath.

LEE. Here?!

TRACY. Of course, here. You want me to take a bath in Sheridan Square?

LEE. Just who the hell are you?

TRACY. Tracy, Tracy Varreta. *I* live here.

PAT. So do we.

LEE. Oh, my God! That dumb agency.

PAT. (*Looking at* TRACY.) They're not so dumb.

LEE. Well, you can't stay here.

TRACY. Now just a minute. I paid my rent.

LEE. But you're a man.

PAT. (*Very Southern.*) You can say that again. Ah may faint.

LEE. They'll just have to refund the rent. I'll get the landlord.

PAT. Forget it. The landlord's name's Simon. One look at Tracy and *we'll* be out on the street.

LEE. Well, what are we gonna do?

TRACY. We're gonna decide who cooks, where we sleep, and what radio station to listen to.

LEE. Where we sleep? (*Points to ottoman.*) Well, you sleep there.

TRACY. Isn't it a little short?

PAT. It's convertible. It opens up into a little, short bed.

TRACY. Why do I have to sleep here?

LEE. (*Patiently.*) Because it's a small apartment with one double bed and the convertible. There are three people. Two women and one man. (*Forcefully, pointing.*) You sleep there!

TRACY. That's sexual discrimination and I heard there will be no sexual discrimination here. (*Pause.*)

PAT. (*Coquettish.*) Well, ah suppose, Tracy, that you will just have to choose one of us.

LEE. Oh, no, he won't. We're not avocados. We'll decide this without reference to sex, impartially, objectively and scientifically.

PAT. How'll we do that?

LEE. We'll draw straws.

PAT. Great. (*To* TRACY.) Got a straw?

TRACY. Not on me. (PAT *is looking for straws.*)

LEE. The short straw gets the convertible.

PAT. I wonder if Simon has any straws.

LEE. The two longer straws get the double bed. I should have stayed in Westchester.

TRACY. You have a lot of straws in Westchester?

PAT. We sure don't have any here. No straws anywhere.

LEE. Of course there are straws. That's how people always settle things. They draw straws.

TRACY. Can we settle this? I'm getting tired of it.

LEE. I don't care how tired you get; no one's sleeping here till we draw straws.

PAT. There aren't any. What do we do now?

LEE. We stay up all night. No straws; no sleep.

TRACY. (*Picks up measurement paper and tears it into strips.*) Okay, this'll do it. Got a pencil?

PAT. (*Who is still holding pencil.*) Yes. (*Gives it to him.*) Here.

TRACY. (*Writing.*) Two Bs and one C. (*Folding them.*) We'll each draw one. The two Bs get each other and C gets the convertible. Ready?

LEE. Maybe we should talk this thing over.

TRACY. (*Holding up the three slips.*) Listen, I'm in a hurry.

PAT. Why?

TRACY. The Giants are playing a game on T.V. tonight.

LEE. That's the last straw. (LEE *and* PAT *each take a slip, leaving* TRACY *holding one.*)

CURTAIN

ACT TWO

Scene 1

The apartment has been slightly refurnished, and is much more attractive. There is a comfortable couch. Amongst the various bric-a-brac, Bernice, the stuffed pig, is fairly prominent. There is a tape player on the bookcase. TRACY is seated, reading and making notes. The tape deck is on very loud. The music should be brassy and classical, probably by Purcell. PAT enters from the bedroom. She is a very Middle European cross between Garbo and Dietrich. She wears spike heels, a belted trench coat with the collar turned up, possibly dark glasses and, definitely, a huge slouch hat. Occasionally she remembers to speak with an ersatz Hungarian accent. She is smoking ostentatiously. She strikes the classic, cliche pose: one leg up on the seat of a chair. TRACY ignores her. She crosses and turns the music off.

PAT. Did you know I vas madly in love with you?

TRACY. (*Deep in the book.*) Yes, you told me yesterday.

PAT. Und I vill probably tell you again tomorrow. A good book? (*No reply.*) Lots of pictures of rats in it? (*No reply.*) What are you reading? (*No reply. Sharply.*) Hein!

TRACY. What?

PAT. We're gonna have to work out a system, Tracy, like secret agents. I'll carry ninety percent of the conversation, talking for both of us, and you can consider most questions rhetorical, but if you hear a twelve second pause at the end of a question and I don't answer myself, that means it's your turn. Okay? Don't answer that. Throw in an occasional grunt when the mood strikes you. It'll help me carry your end of the conversation. I think I wanted to know what you're reading, but it was so long ago, I don't care anymore. You know, it would be easier talking for you if I knew what you were like. I mean, I know you're Tracy Varetta, twenty-five years old, medium height, grey eyes, (*Adjust to fit actor.*) currently doing graduate work in psychology at N.Y.U. But what does it all add up to? Not that I think you're hiding things, you understand. It's very hard to have secrets when the bathtub's in the kitchen. It's just that I want to know who you are. So prepare yourself, 'cos I'm going to ask you a question and pause for twelve seconds. Ready? (*Back into mystery woman part.*) Then I begin. Who are you? (*Very long pause.*) Now for those of you who may not have heard that, I repeat it. Pay attention. There's someone under my skin and I vant to know who it is. (*Long pause,* TRACY *studying.* PAT *shouts.*) Tracy, I want an answer!

TRACY. (*Looking up, startled.*) Clinical Studies of Reaction to Aversive Stimulis in a Deprived Environment.

PAT. What?

TRACY. (*Holding out the book for her to look at.*) That's what I'm reading.

PAT. I'll wait for the movie. (TRACY *goes back to the book.*) You know, I think if we're going to live here in close quarters, we ought to get to know each other better. We should understand each other's moods and feelings. First off, let's consider your feelings. Okay, that's done. Now let's consider mine. You know I'm in love with you. I actually knew it the first day but I didn't tell you then because I was hoping it was just a twenty-four hour virus. Sure enough, it was love. It wasn't even for the right reasons like you were easy to talk to or a producer. I think it was the way the hair grew down the back of your neck and how you brushed your teeth without spattering toothpaste anywhere. (*Mystery woman again.*) Vy don't we do something mad like make hungry sveating love? Doktor, with your mind and my body we can rule the world. Or as we used to say in Lithuania, "Si el tren se para entre la estaciones quedesa adentro." Which translates as . . . (*She pushes his book up against his chest so that he cannot read and has to focus on her.*) . . . Do you love me?

TRACY. No.

PAT. Will you marry me anyway?

TRACY. No.

PAT. (*Brightly.*) Well, I'll try again tomorrow.

TRACY. I like you.

PAT. Thanks a lot. How are the rats?

TRACY. Pretty good. I think my theory is going to hold up. The general apathy has worn off and in the last few days there's been a marked increase in the incidence of cannibalism and incest.

PAT. See, I just knew, once you'd put that book down, we'd have a great conversation. Tell me about your love life.

TRACY. I don't think I have one.

PAT. Of course you do. Everyone has one. They may not be sleeping with anybody, but they do have a love life.

TRACY. I never thought about it.

PAT. You're twenty-five. Start thinking. What type of girl do you like?

TRACY. I don't like types. I like individuals.

PAT. Do you like these individuals to be blonde or brunette?

TRACY. Why?

PAT. Because Simon has dozens of wigs I can borrow. I mean are you looking for a mother, a sex object, or a pal? I do pal very well, but I'll work on mother or sex object if that's what you want. Here I am. What would you like me to be?

TRACY. Quiet.

PAT. What do you think of Lee?

TRACY. She's nice.

PAT. Do you think she's attractive?

TRACY. Yes.

PAT. Very attractive?

TRACY. What do you mean by very?

PAT. Does she turn you on?

TRACY. I'm not a light bulb.

PAT. What are you going to do when you graduate? Open an office?

TRACY. No, I'm going to be a research psychologist.

PAT. No plush office with a leather couch and rich, bored ladies lying on it?

TRACY. No.

PAT. What a shame, I was hoping for a free consultation. If I don't get professional help soon, I don't think I'll make it.

TRACY. You're as healthy as a horse.

PAT. No, I'm not, I know I seem normal, but underneath I'm sick, really sick. (*Who by this time is lying on the couch.*) Tell me, doctor, is it too late for help?

TRACY. I'm not a doctor.

PAT. Would you like to hear about my childhood?

TRACY. Not particularly.

PAT. I have an older sister and a younger brother and my parents loved us all very much. They loved my sister because she was the oldest, and they loved my brother because he was the youngest, and they loved me because there I was in the middle and there wasn't much else they could do with me. (*Beat.*) There, now you can see how it all began.

TRACY. How all what began?

PAT. This craving, this desperate need to be oldest or youngest or something.

TRACY. What do you want anyway?

PAT. What do you mean, what do I want? I wanta know who I am. I wanta find someone else who knows who I am. (*Sincere.*) What does anyone want, love and happiness.

TRACY. (*Quietly.*) Oh.

PAT. (*Brightly.*) That's the first time you've ever really talked to me.

TRACY. I . . . er . . . got carried away.

PAT. It's okay.

TRACY. Maybe you try too hard.

PAT. Maybe. I was just trying to be what you wanted.

TRACY. What's that?

PAT. An in-depth study. Maybe I do try too hard, but you think too much and don't try at all. Anyway, I have no objection to being treated as a sexual object. I think I'd like it. (LEE *enters with shopping bag.*)

LEE. Anybody home?

TRACY. Everybody.

LEE. Macy's is a madhouse, my feet are killing me, and it's starting to rain. I see we got the couch. How'd you get it up here?

TRACY. I got Rocky to help, and Simon gave direction.

LEE. Why didn't Simon help?

PAT. You can't move furniture while your nail polish is still wet.

LEE. Well, now we just have to draw straws to see who sleeps where and not with whom.

PAT. Simon wanted to be in on the next drawing.

TRACY. It's not the New York State Lottery.

LEE. And what does Simon know about it anyway? We agreed not to talk about it.

PAT. He just knows we drew straws. Not who won or lost.

TRACY. *We* don't know who won or lost yet.

LEE. I don't like our sleeping arrangements being discussed with Simon or anyone else. Has Bob called here? (*Disposing shopping in appropriate places.*)

TRACY. Not since the third time last night.

PAT. Why don't you talk to him?

LEE. Because if I'm forever talking to him, it's not any kind of separation or experiment. He called me at school yesterday.

TRACY. He's very suspicious when I answer the phone.

LEE. If he knew that you were Tracy, I'd be in bad trouble.

PAT. Why?

LEE. Because a long, long time ago when the world was young, married women didn't leave home and move in with muscular young psychology students.

PAT. Don't worry about it; this student's interested in theory, not practice.

LEE. Bob really is trying to get in here and find out what's going on.

PAT. Well, if he does, I wish he'd let *me* know what's going on.

LEE. That's enough about Bob. I'm supposed to be away from him. Whose turn was it to take the garbage out?

PAT. Guilty.

LEE. Whose socks? (*Picks them up and tosses them to* TRACY.)

TRACY. Mine.

LEE. You know, I think that's why I left home.

PAT. Which one of you wants to lend me ten dollars?

TRACY. Lee does.

LEE. But only if you take the garbage out.

PAT. I promise.

TRACY. What do you want money for?

PAT. I have a date tonight.

LEE. Then why do you need money?

PAT. He's coming here. I'm going to fix dinner.

TRACY. What're you going to fix?

PAT. Lamb chops.

TRACY. Sounds good. I like lamb.

LEE. I don't think I've ever cooked lamb. Bob hates it. Anyway I'm sort of a hamburger, chicken, and Campbell's soup cook. Maybe I'll watch and learn something.

PAT. Hey, I think there's been a little misunderstanding.

TRACY. How come?

PAT. He's coming here. I'm cooking for the two of us: he and I. Not the four of us. The two of us.

LEE. What are we supposed to do?

PAT. Leave.

TRACY. Now, just a minute . . .

PAT. (*Cutting off.*) We agreed anyone of us could have the apartment for entertaining.

LEE. We were supposed to get advance notice.

PAT. He just asked me this afternoon. Don't come between us and what could turn out to be the second greatest love of my life.

LEE. Who's the first?

TRACY. (*Quickly.*) Okay, we'll leave.

LEE. Who's the date?

PAT. Some guy.

LEE. I assumed that. Where'd you meet him?

PAT. In the drugstore. He's just getting over a divorce. The poor man hasn't had a decent meal in ages. Nothing but bacon and eggs since they split up. Can I have the money now?

LEE. Oh, sure.

TRACY. For a first date he should take you out. He sounds like a cheapskate.

PAT. He is not cheap. He's going to bring the wine. Anyway, he's not a student; he's worldly and mature and he gets what he wants.

LEE. (*Handing the money.*) Here.

PAT. Thanks. (*Crosses to the door.*) After I shop, I'm going by Simon's to pick out a simple, little dress. "La via del Tren subterranes es peligrossa. No salga afuero."

LEE. What's that mean?

PAT. Be out by seven-thirty. (*Garbo.*) Ve vant to be alone. (*Exits.*)

TRACY. Simon's idea of a simple little dress is probably eleven yards of gold lame.

LEE. Dammit!

TRACY. What?

LEE. She forgot the garbage.

TRACY. I'll take it when I leave.

LEE. Where are you going?

TRACY. The library, I guess.

LEE. I really didn't want to go anywhere. I wanted to take my shoes off, put my feet up, and watch T.V. Trust Pat to change that. What do you think of Pat?

TRACY. She's nice.

LEE. Do you think she's attractive?

TRACY. I've never really seen her. Just caricatures of Scarlett O'Hara and the Tooth Fairy.

LEE. That was supposed to be Florence Nightingale.

TRACY. Whatever.

LEE. Who is your dream girl?

TRACY. I dunno.

LEE. Julie Andrews or Jane Fonda?

TRACY. Neither. Just a girl. You know, brown hair, glasses and a plaid skirt.

LEE. That's nice, but it's not Pat.

TRACY. I don't really know Pat.

LEE. I wonder how well anybody ever knows anybody else. You can even sleep with them and not know them. I'm not sure that I know Bob.

TRACY. Why won't you talk to him?

LEE. I will talk to him. I'm just not ready yet.

TRACY. When are you going to be ready?

LEE. I don't know. But don't worry, it's fated Bob and I will meet again. (*Grim.*) And then we'll see who's a dumb vampire. Do you want a drink?

TRACY. Sure. (LEE *fixes drinks.*) Why did you leave him?

LEE. You mean apart from the fact that he left his socks, and newspapers, and empty Pepsi glasses around for me to pick up?

TRACY. Yeah, leave the socks out of it.

LEE. (*Handing him a drink.*) I think it was the magazines.

TRACY. What magazines?

LEE. Time, Newsweek, all of them. They kept telling

me about my life style, which changed weekly. One week I was supposed to be eating natural foods, the next having an affair. Then there was group therapy week, orgy week, and social involvement week. Life styles were just zipping by me and there I was, doing none of them. I think I made my decision to leave the week I read Family Circle and found out I was the only one left who couldn't grow African Violets.

TRACY. Those magazines have to have something to write about.

LEE. But they weren't writing about me. Same with the movies.

TRACY. You were bored.

LEE. Not just bored, guilty. If you read enough of that stuff, you finally feel guilty for not doing it, whatever it is. So here I am.

TRACY. How do you like it?

LEE. I like it. I might not like it for long, but right now, I like it.

TRACY. Maybe you'll stay.

LEE. I doubt it. The real me belongs in a nice suburban home with a nice family. That's what I really want, I guess. But, and this is important, I want it to be my decision, based on a choice. I don't want it to be the only option. (*Tiny pause.*) Wow, I've never said all that before.

TRACY. Maybe you should've said it to Bob.

LEE. I'm not sure I knew it, till just now. Tell me about you.

TRACY. There's nothing to tell. I grew up and went to school. I'm still there.

LEE. There must be something under that cool exterior. Do you dance?

TRACY. Yes.

LEE. That's something. Bob hates dancing. What else do you like doing?

TRACY. I like movies and plays. Reading. And I like walking.

LEE. Walking?

TRACY. Yes. Sunday mornings in the park or down by the river. But especially at night, after a rain.

LEE. Where did you say you were going?

TRACY. The school library. And you?

LEE. I don't know. Do you have to finish something tonight?

TRACY. No, why?

LEE. I thought since we've been temporarily evicted, we might go somewhere together.

TRACY. Are you asking me for a date?

LEE. Why not? I'm a liberated woman with a tongue in my head. There's no reason for me to go out alone.

TRACY. Where would we go?

LEE. Out. Out dining, and drinking, and dancing.

TRACY. And walking?

LEE. And walking. You'll go?

TRACY. Sure. I like a free meal.

LEE. What d'you mean, free?

TRACY. Well, you asked me for a date. That means you're paying. Liberation cuts both ways. I think I'd like lobster.

LEE. (*Cool.*) Should I bring you a present?

TRACY. That'd be nice. Nothing personal. Flowers or candy. Mother said never accept personal gifts on a first date.

LEE. I never thought I'd seriously be asking a man out for dinner. I mean for a date. Marriage eliminated that possibility. I was . . .

TRACY. Safe.

LEE. Yes. Now there's a whole new set of rules. Or maybe no rules.

TRACY. Nervous?

LEE. A little.

TRACY. Don't be. It's easy. Take it one step at a time. Just like walking.

CURTAIN

ACT TWO

SCENE 2

BOB *and* PAT *are sitting at the table, over the remains of dinner. She is wearing a classic early Thirties, floor-length sheath, and an ostrich feather boa. There is one empty wine bottle and a full one newly opened. A long pause. Finally,* BOB *takes out cigarettes, offers one to* PAT *who smiles weakly and shakes her head, and lights his own. Another long pause.* PAT *drains her wine glass. She picks up the bottle, looks inquiringly at* BOB *who nods, and fills both glasses.* BOB *clears his throat as if about to speak, but doesn't. A pause long enough to scare Pinter into dialogue. Then . . .*

BOB. When did you first know who I really am?

PAT. As soon as you got here.

BOB. How was that?

PAT. You came in and said, "Where's Lee?" before you even said hello.

BOB. Oh. (*Pause. They finish the wine.* BOB *picks up the bottle, looks inquiringly at* PAT, *who nods, and refills both glasses, emptying the bottle.*)

PAT. Are you going to wait till they get back?

BOB. I don't know. Do you know why she left?

PAT. She said something about socks.

BOB. Yeah, I know what she means. I didn't use to, but this morning the only way into the kitchen was over newspapers and socks.

PAT. Why don't you pick them up?

BOB. They stop the carpet getting dirty. This way I don't have to vacuum. How is Lee as a roommate?

PAT. She's fine.

BOB. And er . . . what's the other girl's name?

PAT. What other girl?

BOB. Your other roommate.

PAT. Oh. Tracy?

BOB. Yeah. How is she as a roommate?

PAT. Fine.

BOB. Good.

PAT. (*Beat.*) There's something I ought to tell you about Tracy.

BOB. No, tell me about Lee. Does she go out much? I mean date? You know, whatever?

PAT. No, I think tonight's the first time.

BOB. Tonight?

PAT. She and Tracy.

BOB. Yeah, but that's just roommates. I didn't mean that. That's okay. Where'd they go?

PAT. Out to eat, and then walking.

BOB. Walking where?

PAT. Just around. Tracy likes walking.

BOB. What does she do? Secretary, actress?

PAT. Student. Psychology.

BOB. I've been reading some psychology lately, to see if I could understand what's happening to Lee and me, and everybody else.

PAT. Did you?

BOB. No. Even the experts don't know. Some of them say there's been a major sexual revolution and some of them say there hasn't.

PAT. What do you think?

BOB. I think there's been a relatively small sexual revolution and a huge revolution in attitudes. Nobody says the word "adultery" with shock or surprise anymore, which is probably good, but it doesn't prepare them for the shock and surprise of finding out adultery has broken up their home.

PAT. And what about love?

BOB. What?

PAT. What have they found out about love?

BOB. Nothing yet. (*Pause.*) That's a pretty outfit.

PAT. It's just a simple, little dress I borrowed from a friend. It looks better on him.

BOB. (*After a tiny pause. With an effort.*) Well, it was a great dinner.

PAT. Thanks.

BOB. I mean it. Its just that I never eat lamb. Lee doesn't cook lamb. She's a very . . . straightforward cook.

PAT. I gather Lee doesn't want to talk to you?

BOB. That's okay. I don't want her to talk to me. I want her to sit quietly with her liberated mouth shut while I talk to her. (*Grim.*) And have I got some things to tell her.

PAT. So that's why you're here?

BOB. That's what I told you, I don't know. I mean, technically I guess I'm here because she said I couldn't come here. But why what she says should matter so much, I don't know. (*Drinks.*) Say, are you mad because I'm not who I said? I messed up your evening; you could've had a real date.

PAT. It doesn't matter. I have problems of my own.

BOB. You do? What?

PAT. I'm in love with Tracy.

BOB. (*Tiny pause.*) Well, it takes all kinds.

PAT. What?

BOB. Don't worry. I'm liberal. Some of my best friends are . . . I never would've guessed . . . I mean, you don't look it.

PAT. Tracy's a guy.

BOB. That's terrific.

PAT. Well, it's going to be a relief to my mother.

BOB. What?

PAT. That he's a guy.

BOB. Yeah. Better for you too.

PAT. All along you thought Tracy was a girl.

BOB. But she's not.

PAT. She's a guy.

BOB. (*Joining in.*) She's a guy. (*Pause.*) Something just occurred to me. What's this guy doing out with my wife?

PAT. They have a date.

BOB. A date! He can't go around asking married women for dates; especially my married women.

PAT. They're only walking.

BOB. That's not the point. He shouldn't ask.

PAT. He didn't ask her. She asked him.

BOB. No, she didn't.

PAT. Yes, she did.

BOB. (*Incredulous.*) She asked him?

PAT. Yep.

BOB. My wife's a very attractive woman, why didn't he ask her?

PAT. Well, I . . .

BOB. Is he blind?

PAT. I . . . er . . .

BOB. Isn't she good enough for him? Or is there something wrong with this guy?

PAT. There's nothing wrong with him.

BOB. How do you know?

PAT. I just know.

BOB. Well, he's got a lot of nerve. If he's gonna run around with married women, why can't he do it straight out like any other regular, red-blooded, all-American heel. If she's gonna cheat, she should cheat with someone I can punch.

PAT. You can punch Tracy. In fact, that's not a bad idea.

BOB. You can't punch a guy who waits to be asked. (*Indicating bedroom.*) Is there a lock on that door?

PAT. There isn't a door. Why?

BOB. Well, he sleeps here, right?

PAT. He does now.

BOB. What do you mean 'now'?

PAT. Now we've got the couch.

BOB. When did you get the couch?

PAT. Today.

BOB. You've been here a week!

PAT. Eight days.

Bob. That's worse. Where'd he sleep, in the bathtub?

Pat. No, of course not. The faucet leaks; he might've drowned.

Bob. He may wish he had.

Pat. The ottoman makes into a bed.

Bob. Thank God.

Pat. But it isn't very comfortable, and it didn't seem fair to make him sleep there, just cos he's a guy, so we drew straws.

Bob. You what?

Pat. Drew straws. Like in Oliver Twist.

Bob. Straws?

Pat. To see who slept where.

Bob. And, consequently, with whom.

Pat. Yep.

Bob. Who won?

Pat. What do you consider winning?

Bob. Who slept with whom?

Pat. We agreed never to tell anyone.

Bob. I'm not anyone. I'm her husband.

Pat. Well, she doesn't want you to know.

Bob. That she's having an affair with a roommate?

Pat. She also doesn't want you to know that she's not having an affair with her roommate. Either way.

Bob. What does she want?

Pat. I don't know.

Bob. (*Having discovered that both wine bottles are empty.*) Well, I know what I want.

Pat. What's that?

Bob. A strong drink. (*Goes to bar to fix it.*)

Pat. Me, too.

Bob. Why, your wife's not liberated?

Pat. No, he's out with another woman.

Bob. Walking?

Pat. Yep.

Bob. There has been a revolution. We used to go to the drive-in. (*Hands her drink.*) Here.

Pat. Thanks.

BOB. What shall we drink to? Roommates, husbands, wives, love?

PAT. Love.

BOB. We gotta know what we're drinking to. What is it?

PAT. Love—makes the world go round. (*Drinks.*)

BOB. It's what the world needs now. (*Drinks.*)

PAT. Love conquers all. (*Drinks.*)

BOB. Love is blind. (*Drinks.*)

PAT. All love is sweet.

BOB. Yeah, but some of it's fattening and some is dietetic.

PAT. Love is like the wild rose briar.

BOB. No, it's not.

PAT. Emily Bronte said it was.

BOB. Well, she obviously didn't know New York. There isn't a rose briar in miles, and if there was, Lee couldn't cook it.

PAT. (*Hiccoughs.*) Sorry.

BOB. Love means never having to say you're sorry. Whatever that means. (*Drinks.*)

PAT. Love is a many flavored thing. (*Drinks.*)

BOB. Love is a four letter word. (*Drinks. They refill from the bottle as needed.*)

PAT. So is pork. (*Drinks.*)

BOB. I'll drink to that. (*Drinks.*)

PAT. (*Simply and sincerely.*) Love is a man and woman, beautifully dressed, on a moonlit balcony overlooking the Riviera, and a small orchestra playing "Someday I'll Find You."

BOB. What?

PAT. It's a scene from Private Lives.

BOB. What's that?

PAT. It's a play about two people who can't live with one another, and can't live without one another.

BOB. Sounds familiar.

PAT. I think we're going to get drunk, if we drink any more.

BOB. I think we may not have to drink any more.

PAT. I think you may be right.

BOB. Love is a tuna casserole. (*Drinks.*)

PAT. What?

BOB. Tuna casserole. I don't think there's a wife that doesn't cook it, or a husband who doesn't hate it; it's put in the oven at three hundred and fifty degrees with phone bills, who's going to take the car in to be serviced, unmowed lawns, the adventures of the divorced neurotic next door, and garlic salt. I've been served that dish every week of my marriage, but one.

PAT. What week was that?

BOB. Last week.

PAT. What did you eat?

BOB. Bacon and eggs.

PAT. I like bacon and eggs.

BOB. (*Sincerely.*) I missed the tuna casserole.

PAT. (*Filling both their glasses.*) To love—whatever it is.

BOB. That says it. (*Both drink.*)

PAT. Well, what do you want to do now?

BOB. I want to make her miserable. That'll show her I love her.

PAT. I want Tracy to suffer.

BOB. I want her to be miserable and suffer.

PAT. I want Tracy to be very miserable and suffer horribly.

BOB. I want all that and also agony.

PAT. I want to cut off his head with a meataxe.

BOB. (*Genuinely shocked.*) That's a terrible thing to say!

PAT. That's what Elyot told Amanda.

BOB. Who are they?

PAT. In Private Lives.

BOB. I hope she hit him.

PAT. She did, later.

BOB. Good for her.

PAT. Then he hit her back.

BOB. Who won?

PAT. They were rolling about the floor fighting when her husband and his wife walked in.

BOB. And then?

PAT. The curtain fell.

BOB. They always cut out the best bits. (*They are both very drunk.*)

PAT. They're gonna be home soon.

BOB. Good. Then we can punch Tracy.

PAT. Do you want them to find you here?

BOB. No. I'll pretend I'm someone else.

PAT. Who?

BOB. (*Sitting, seriously.*) Your mother.

PAT. Wouldn't work.

BOB. Why not?

PAT. My mother doesn't shave.

BOB. Oh.

PAT. They're going to come in from their date and find us just sitting here, looking silly.

BOB. That's an awful thing to say to your mother.

PAT. What do you really want from Lee? An end to this separation, a reconciliation based on affection and mutual respect, a new beginning or revenge?

BOB. I'm a civilized person, you know, not an animal. Naturally, I want revenge.

PAT. Good. We'll do the second act of Private Lives.

BOB. Do you think they'll care if they find us fighting?

PAT. No. But we needn't be fighting.

BOB. We could be kissing.

PAT. That's it; making love.

BOB. No, kissing.

PAT. All right now let me see, I'll be here on the couch like this. (*She is directing them into position.*) Now you be round here, no, turn this way. Sort of . . .

BOB. It's awkward.

PAT. It's supposed to be romantic, not comfortable. Now put that hand on the back of the couch. Now lean down, and I'll put this arm round the back of your neck.

There. (*They are in a supposedly romantic, but hard to hold pose.*)

BOB. Is this it?

PAT. This is it. (*Pause.*)

BOB. God, I hope they come in soon.

PAT. I like your smile. That's very good.

BOB. It's not a smile; I'm gritting my teeth.

PAT. Why?

BOB. Because my arm's gone to sleep. Are you sure this is romantic? It doesn't feel like it.

PAT. (*Crawling awkwardly out of position, so as not to move BOB.*) Stay there and I'll go and see. (*Crosses to front door.*) Now they're gonna come in here, and see . . . Tilt your head a bit more. No, the other way. Let's see, I'm sort of there like this . . . (*She is twisting around, visualizing her own position.*) . . . with one arm . . . the other arm . . . yes, that looks great. (*She crosses back and crawls back into position.*)

BOB. I think it might be easier if I just flew to Haiti and got a divorce.

PAT. Don't be cynical. Look sophisticated.

BOB. I can't. It hurts too much.

PAT. Okay. We're all set. Now, say something passionate.

BOB. What?

PAT. Say something passionate.

BOB. (*Long pause.*) I don't know anything passionate.

PAT. No wonder Lee left. (*Crawling out again.*) Now I want you to think elegant, and romantic. (*Cutting off main overhead light, leaving on a lamp.*) Imagine candlelight and moonlight. And soft music. Strange how potent cheap music is. (*She switches on radio or tape deck. Instantly the music TRACY was listening to in the previous scene blares out so loudly as to nearly knock her down. She adjusts it to something soft and romantic.*)

BOB. And loud.

PAT. That's better. (*Crawling back onto couch this time feet first over the arm.*) Okay, now are you getting in the mood? Think beautiful, poetic thoughts. It needn't be original. Use a piece of poetry if you have to. On your mark, get ready, set. Say something romantic and passionate. (*There is a pause.*)

BOB. (*Gently.*)
"By the shores of Gitche Gumee
 By the shining Big-Sea-Water . . ."

PAT. (*Screams.*) No! Forget it. (BOB *collapses on top of her.*) Ouch!

BOB. (*As they are untangling.*) Don't make me go back there. Please don't make me.

PAT. We're gonna start over. You lie on the couch where I was, and I'll sit on the arm. (*Getting in position.*)

BOB. Do you think this will work?

PAT. We're going to do it till we get it right.

BOB. What if they come home before we're ready?

PAT. They'll just have to go out again and wait till we are. (*They are now in the reverse position.*)

BOB. Now say something passionate.

PAT. (*It really sounds good.*) Si el tren se para entre la estaciones no salga afuero.

BOB. That's beautiful. What does it mean?

PAT. It's an old Spanish poem, about a lover and his faithless mistress. He begs her to return before the orange blossoms fall. They first met in an orange orchard and he wooed her with melodies on his mandolin and for a while they were happy, but he was poor and she was beautiful so eventually she met a Castilian nobleman of ancient lineage, and went with him to his castle, where there were no orange groves so she was unhappy, but remembering her mother's prophecy she stained her skin with walnut juice and (*Realizing he's asleep.*) Wake up!

BOB. What?

PAT. I was translating.

BOB. It means all that?!

PAT. Nearly all that.

BOB. Where are they? They should be back now.

PAT. Maybe it won't work. (*Gets up.*)

BOB. Let's have another drink while we're waiting. (*Fixes them.*)

PAT. They may walk in and catch us drinking.

BOB. Maybe we'll hear them coming.

PAT. You can't hear through the door.

BOB. Maybe if we were in the other room, we'd have a chance to hear them and get ready.

PAT. That's the bedroom.

BOB. We could just be doing what we were doing in here.

PAT. On the couch it's romantic; in the bedroom it's just dirty.

BOB. Let's give up.

PAT. I've got it! The balcony. There's a balcony outside our bedroom window that connects with Simon's. They'll get back, one of them at least will come into the bedroom and there we'll be, silhouetted against moonlight, embracing.

BOB. Shock!

PAT. Revenge!

BOB. And curtain! (*They exit to the bedroom. Pause, BOB re-enters and gets both drinks. Exits. PAT re-enters and gets her ostrich feathers. Exits. BOB re-enters and gets the bottle. Exits. TRACY and LEE enter through the front door. They are dressed for a night out and make a glamorous couple, coming much closer to Private Lives than BOB and PAT.*)

LEE. I had no idea walking could be so much fun.

TRACY. I do it all the time. It's easy, relaxing, cheap . . .

LEE. And wonderful. All those little shops and the violinist playing on the corner. I loved it. And the restaurant was . . . perfect. It's been a beautiful evening. But it's rather awkward now.

TRACY. Why?

LEE. Because we're roommates. And we have a third roommate who's in love with you.

TRACY. It's a part she plays. She's not really.

LEE. Don't be so sure. Anyway, it's damned awkward. (*Slowly and naturally, they drift into a similar romantic pose to that which* PAT *and* BOB *struggled to maintain, but for* LEE *and* TRACY *it is easy and graceful. The position should not be completed until two lines before the curtain.*)

TRACY. Rise above it.

LEE. You look relaxed.

TRACY. I am.

LEE. That's not very flattering.

TRACY. Remember, the initiative's yours. You asked me out ·. . .

LEE. I don't know how to make up my mind.

TRACY. Draw straws. (LEE *kisses* TRACY. *At that moment, so drunk they have to support each other,* PAT *and* BOB *enter from the bedroom.*)

BOB. That's not how the second act ends!

CURTAIN

ACT THREE

Early the next morning. The debris of the night before remains pretty much as it was. A couple of rumpled blankets, PAT'S *feather boa and a pillow are on the couch. The ottoman, as always, is closed up.* TRACY, *wearing a bathrobe, is pouring himself some orange juice.* LEE, *wearing a bathrobe, enters from the bedroom.*

LEE. Good morning. Isn't it a wonderful morning?

TRACY. How can you tell?

LEE. If you can see all seven fire-escapes, it means that somewhere out there the sun is shining.

TRACY. Juice?

LEE. (*He pours her some.*) Please.

TRACY. It's early on a Sunday morning and everybody's up. We must be crazy. Maybe it's because of last night.

LEE. I loved last night.

TRACY. All of it?

LEE. All of it. And now it's a wonderful morning; crisp and sunny and I'm in love.

TRACY. Can you wait till I finish my juice.

LEE. With Bob.

TRACY. Bob who?

LEE. What do you mean, Bob who? Bob—Bob, my husband, Bob.

TRACY. Is that the same Bob you wouldn't speak to last night?

LEE. Yes.

TRACY. The Bob you told me to throw out as you stormed into the bedroom, that Bob?

LEE. Him. We're in love.

TRACY. Boy, is he in for a surprise.

49

LEE. I can't wait to see him.

TRACY. (*Startled.*) Right now?

LEE. Oh, no. He'll have an awful hangover. He always does. He needs to wake up slowly and gently. I'll phone him this afternoon.

TRACY. Good idea.

LEE. This place is an incredible mess.

TRACY. I think it's a reflection of the people who live here.

LEE. Where's Pat?

TRACY. I don't know.

LEE. She'll probably burst in soon.

TRACY. As whom?

LEE. Does it matter?

TRACY. Maybe.

LEE. Well, I want Bob, and you and Pat will just have to work it out.

TRACY. Why do we have to work anything out? Used to be a guy and a girl couldn't live together, well now they can, and what's more they don't *have* to sleep together.

LEE. Yeah, well they better have a bigger apartment than this. You know, I really wanted a change from Westchester, but I'm not sure this is what I had in mind. I was sort of hoping for something more . . . exotic.

TRACY. What do you call exotic?

LEE. Well, I used to call Tibet exotic, but right now, I'd settle for a tiled bathroom. (PAT *bursts in the front door carrying a coffee pot. She is dressed in a musical-comedy sailor outfit and is very, very pregnant . . .*)

PAT. Out of your hammocks, m' hearties.

LEE. I take it back. This place is exotic.

TRACY. Well, now we know what they did with the drunken sailor.

PAT. I was not drunk; I was a little tipsy. Simon sent hot coffee.

LEE. Good. I was just about to make some.

PAT. Anything to eat?

LEE. I think there's some Danish.

PAT. (*Fixing coffee.*) How many coffees?

TRACY. Three.

LEE. Pat, I wouldn't dream of asking about the sailor suit; I'm sure there's a perfectly commonplace answer, but why pregnant?

PAT. Ask Tracy.

TRACY. It's not mine!

LEE. (*To* PAT.) Why didn't you fold up your blankets?

PAT. I tried, but I wasn't feeling too well. I must have eaten too much.

TRACY. (*Crossing to the bedroom door.*) Well, I'm gonna go get dressed.

PAT. I'll straighten up the bedroom.

TRACY. (*Exits to bedroom.*) Fold your blankets.

LEE. I suppose we'd better clean up.

PAT. I guess last night was pretty messy. What'll we do?

LEE. Start with the blankets, and I'll get the dishes. (*They are straightening up during the scene.*) No, I mean about last night.

LEE. I had a great time.

PAT. Listen, it was all a mistake. I had no idea it was Bob until it was too late; till he was here. When I woke up this morning I felt awful.

LEE. You probably ate too much.

PAT. Not that kind of awful. And that part in the bedroom, when we were in the bedroom and you and Tracy were out here, and it looked like . . . well, what we planned was . . . what we were doing was . . . I mean we weren't doing anything, honest.

LEE. Of course not.

PAT. You shouldn't feel that way. Nowadays just because two people are drunk in a bedroom together doesn't mean anything. Of course, it means something, but not anything like the something someone who saw anyone doing something like that might think.

LEE. You mean fooling around?

PAT. Something like that.

LEE. Couldn't you at least have scraped the plates?

PAT. Let me put it like this: I don't really like Bob.

LEE. (*Indignant.*) What do you mean?

PAT. I mean, I do *like* him, but that's it. I mean he's very nice. Warm, intelligent, handsome, amusing, but he's not my type.

LEE. What's your type.

PAT. When I've spent hours cleaning the apartment, getting dressed, and cooking a great dinner, my type eats it.

LEE. He's never liked lamb.

PAT. All things considered, Bob and I had a miserable time. How was your date with Tracy?

LEE. Wonderful. I loved it.

PAT. That's not fair.

LEE. We went to this tiny little restaurant that only had five tables but the most delicious food in the world.

PAT. Did you go dancing?

LEE. No, afterwards we went walking and later we stopped for a drink at this place where they had a trio playing, and when I woke up this morning, I realized I was in love.

PAT. (*Glum.*) You're years older than him.

LEE. No, I'm not.

PAT. Who are you talking about?

LEE. Bob, of course. Who else?

PAT. Congratulations! How did that happen?

LEE. I don't know . . . I guess anybody who phones me twenty times a day and goes to elaborate lengths to get into my apartment is obviously no longer taking me for granted. (TRACY *enters from the bedroom, dressed.*)

TRACY. Well, I timed that nicely. You've got everything straightened up.

LEE. (*Taking the last thing from the table, the ice-bucket and putting it on a shelf.*) We've still got the dishes to wash.

PAT. You'd better empty that. It's probably full of melted ice.

TRACY. (*Quickly.*) No, it isn't.

LEE. (*Checking.*) Yes, it is. (*Crosses to the tub.*)

TRACY. Well, let's leave the dishes and things till later. It's Sunday morning, a beautiful day. Let's go somewhere.

PAT. Where?

TRACY. I dunno. We could ride the ferry.

PAT. Yeah.

LEE. (*Cleaning off anything that's on the tub.*) I don't think I want to go out. Bob may call and if he doesn't, I'm going to phone him in a bit.

PAT. (*To* TRACY.) Isn't it great about Lee and Bob?

TRACY. (*Very unenthusiastic.*) Great.

LEE. (*Raising the tub lid.*) I hope he got home all right. He was terribly drunk. I'd hate to wake him up too early. (*She empties the icebucket into the tub. There is a shout.* BOB *appears over the edge of the tub, tousled, half-asleep, very hung-over and recently wet.*)

BOB. Bail like hell, we're sinking!

LEE. (*To* PAT.) Why didn't you tell me he was in there?

PAT. I didn't know. I don't remember going to bed myself.

BOB. Good morning, dear. Has the paper come?

LEE. (*To* TRACY.) I thought when I went to bed I told you to put him out.

TRACY. You couldn't put a dog out in that condition.

LEE. (*Distracted.*) Dog, no; Bob, yes.

PAT. I thought the faucet dripped.

BOB. Don't worry, it still drips. (*He climbs out.*)

TRACY. You want some coffee?

BOB. Yes, please.

PAT. Do you need some dry clothes? I could get a dress from Simon and you could wear this.

BOB. No thanks. I think I'm too old to have a baby.

TRACY. What do you want in it?

Bob. A little milk and two alka-seltzer. (Lee *gets a towel and dries his hair.*)

Pat. (*Taking the blankets from the tub and tossing them on his lap.*) We all have to fold our own blankets.

Bob. (*Looking at his hands.*) There's no feeling in my blankets.

Lee. Get a grip on yourself.

Bob. If I could get a grip on anything, I'd fold up the blankets.

Lee. (*Chidingly.*) Serves you right. You know you can't hold liquor.

Bob. Yeah, well God's punishing me, because now I can't even hold blankets. Maybe I'm trying too hard. Do you have a sheet I could practice on?

Lee. How do you feel now?

Bob. My socks are wet.

Lee. (*Taking off his socks and drying his feet. To* Tracy.) Why didn't you tell me he was there?

Tracy. Last night you wanted him out. This morning you wanted him to sleep. I didn't know what to do.

Pat. (*To* Bob.) Would you like to ride the ferry?

Bob. Only if it's going to sink.

Tracy. How about something to eat?

Bob. What have you got?

Pat. There's some left over artichokes.

Bob. I guess I'm not really hungry.

Lee. (*Concerned.*) What do you want?

Bob. I think I just want to sit very, very still.

Lee. Well, you do that. You can have the sofa all to yourself. Would you like to read the paper?

Tracy. I'll go get it.

Bob. No hurry. I'm going to have to learn to read all over again.

Pat. (*Crossing to the radio or tape deck.*) I know exactly how you feel. Sometimes I'm just not in the mood to read especially if it's the Red Badge of Courage. This'll cheer you up. (*Switches on the radio. Instantly we hear a group belting a very militant hymn very loudly. It might be neat if it were the Holy City, but anything forceful will do.* BOB *nearly dies.* TRACY *immediately switches the radio off.*)

TRACY. Are you crazy?

BOB. (*After a beat, to* LEE.) Darling, I know it's all over between us, but for old times sake, please . . . don't let her do that again.

LEE. I won't. You just sit there, now. (*To* PAT.) How could you?

PAT. I thought it'd help.

TRACY. He wants to be soothed, not saved.

LEE. Well, once he's a little better, we'll go home where it's quiet.

TRACY. (*To* LEE.) You'd better drive.

LEE. Maybe he came down by train.

PAT. No, last night he said he parked on Waverly.

LEE. I'd better drive.

PAT. (*To* TRACY.) You want to get a new roommate from the agency, or put up a notice in the drugstore?

TRACY. Let's think about it. There's no rush.

LEE. The rent's paid for this month. You might as well enjoy it. With only two of you, this place is simply . . .

TRACY. Crowded?

LEE. Yes.

PAT. It's not really crowded; it's just sociable.

LEE. I cannot wait to take a long, hot, private shower.

PAT. Maybe Roger wants to move back in?

LEE. Did he pay his rent?

PAT. Yes.

TRACY. I dunno what the rush is. It's only Sunday and Lee hasn't left yet.

LEE. Well, don't worry about that, Lee Schallert is on her way. And after she's taken that shower, she's gonna get out a can of tuna and a can of Campbell's and go to work.

PAT. I bet your place is a mess

LEE. Probably, but if you get up every morning and make it to work and fight your way home through the rush hour, you don't want to vacuum, you want to grab a beer and watch T.V. It wasn't till this past week, working every day, that I realized that. So, I'm a-going back!

BOB. Lee.

LEE. Yes dear?

BOB. I realized something, too.

LEE. What's that?

BOB. You know you said, well shouted actually, that I didn't know if I wanted you back or not?

LEE. Yes?

BOB. Well, maybe you were right after all.

LEE. (*Hugging him.*) I knew you'd see it my way.

TRACY. I don't think that's what he means.

LEE. (*To* BOB.) What do you mean?

BOB. I'm not sure I want you back.

LEE. What?

PAT. He's not sure he wants you back.

LEE. But that's ridiculous. I'm ready to come home.

BOB. (*Finally getting up.*) Well, goody, goody. The prodigal wife returns. What am I supposed to do, kill the fatted tuna?

LEE. What do you mean?

BOB. I mean you got a little bored, didn't you? You were unfulfilled? Well, I have news for you: we're all unfulfilled. The last fulfilled person I know of was St. Catherine and they got her for it.

LEE. But . . . but you kept calling, and coming here?

BOB. That was so we could talk it out, but you didn't need to talk it out. You made all the decisions like leaving without a warning and coming back without a word. I've been eating bacon and eggs and canned ravioli, but now that I've caught double-pneumonia from the Chinese water torture, it's all over and you're graciously coming back to open cans for me. Do you think I've been in a monastery while you've been down here drawing straws for beds or whatever? Well, I haven't. Just how do you know I haven't got an attractive young secretary named Shirley coming by to grill me a steak? How do you know

I'm not keeping three luscious broads and an Arab dancer in Westchester County?

LEE. They don't allow Arabs in Westchester. It's very exclusive.

BOB. So's Shirley. And I don't think I need you anymore; while you were gone, I bought an electric can-opener.

LEE. (*Seething; a virago.*) La via del tren subterraneo es peligrossa. Si el tren se para entre la estaciones que-dessa adentro. No salga afuero! !

BOB. (*Beat.*) What's that mean?

LEE. (*Beat.*) Ask Pat.

PAT. (*Uneasy.*) It . . . er . . . means . . .

TRACY. (*Warning.*) The truth.

PAT. Subway tracks are dangerous. If the train stops between stations, stay inside. Do not get out.

BOB. (*Beat, then viciously to* LEE.) Same to you!

TRACY. (*After a fractional pause, quickly.*) I think I'll run downstairs and get the paper.

PAT. (*Starting toward him.*) I'll help you carry it.

TRACY. (*Dry.*) I think I can manage. (*Exits front door.*)

PAT. (*Hopelessly.*) Anyone want anything?

LEE. A divorce lawyer.

PAT. I think I'll make the bed. (*Exits to bedroom.*)

LEE. I'm going to leave here.

BOB. Whatsa matter, not getting enough variety from drawing those straws? Or is Tracy more interested in Pat?

LEE. And I'm not going to tell you where I'm going. So let me warn you that if you give Miriam five martinis, all you'll get out of her is hiccoughs.

BOB. That's more than I've got out of you lately.

LEE. Please leave, so I can pack.

BOB. Don't let me stop you. Go right ahead. Pack up all your cares and woes and move again. That's a really terrific way of solving your problems.

LEE. Are you going to leave or not?

BOB. I'm not ready to leave yet. My head still hurts.

LEE. Good.

BOB. And my socks are still wet.

LEE. (*Getting a suitcase, which is somewhere in the living room, and opening it on the couch.*) Listen, I have lots of things to do, so please don't bother me by speaking.

BOB. Well, if Tracy brings me the sports section. I won't say a word.

LEE. That would make it just like old times. You reading about basketball, me slaving over a hot stove, and never the twain shall meet.

BOB. We met; we met. Remember after the Ferguson's party, we met that night. My God, we met.

LEE. That was six months ago.

BOB. Well, they'll probably have another party soon.

LEE. I'm talking about you meeting me as a person. You think everything can be smoothed over by a few smutty jokes. Well, it can't.

BOB. How many smutty jokes does it take?

PAT. (*Entering from the bedroom. Brightly.*) I made the bed.

LEE. (*Who, by chance, happens to be near or focused on* PAT, *to* BOB.) You are a self-indulgent, inconsiderate, lazy slob.

PAT. (*Quietly.*) I think I'll change the sheets. (*Exits to bedroom.*)

BOB. I am not self-indulgent, inconsiderate, or lazy.

LEE. You left out something.

BOB. Okay, maybe I am a slob, but I'm a considerate, hard-working slob, and you knew that when you married me. Anyway, nobody's perfect; for instance, you're a rotten cook.

LEE. Of course I'm a rotten cook; I'm married to a man who likes two things: hamburger meat and Rice Krispies.

BOB. That's not true. I like lots of other things.

LEE. Such as?

BOB. Well . . . I like milk on my Rice Krispies.

LEE. And pajamas.

BOB. I don't like milk on my pajamas.

LEE. You still wear pajamas in bed.

BOB. Yeah, well, it stops my suit from getting wrinkled.

LEE. Four year old boys and men on social security wear pajamas; you are the last man your age who wears pajamas.

BOB. I'd better rush right over to Sears and tell them; they've got whole departments full of pajamas.

LEE. That's not what I meant. It's not romantic.

BOB. You mean Burt Reynolds doesn't wear pajamas? Of course not, if I looked like Burt Reynolds, neither would I. Believe me, I'm more romantic in pajamas.

LEE. Tracy doesn't wear pajamas.

BOB. (*Furious.*) That does it! I don't give a damn what that student hustler wears in bed, and what's more neither should you.

LEE. Don't be so old-fashioned. (*The buzzer for the front door rings. Neither of them pay any attention.*)

BOB. Let me tell you how old-fashioned I'm gonna be. I'm gonna put you over my knee and paddle some sense into you. That's how old-fashioned.

LEE. That's ridiculous.

BOB. Yeah, well this ridiculous, old-fashioned, slob is tired of being told he's a ridiculous, old-fashioned, slob by his smart-mouthed wife.

LEE. (*As he begins to stalk her.*) Don't you come near me.

BOB. (*Who is enjoying this.*) See the slob from Westchester invade Greenwich Village. The Slob is coming.

LEE. (*Backing off.*) If you touch me, I'll scream.

BOB. Who do you think's going to rescue you, the pregnant sailor, or the dumb vampire upstairs? (*Uses a Dracula voice.*) You seem so full of life, my dear.

LEE. That's a terrible Boris Karloff, and if you don't stop I'll . . . I'll . . . sprinkle you with garlic.

BOB. (*Dracula voice.*) The dreaded Slob. He doesn't bite your neck; he smacks your bottom.

LEE. (*Rummaging through the spices.*) I don't suppose you're allergic to nutmeg or vanilla extract?

BOB. (*Dracula voice.*) And everywhere the Slob goes, he leaves a trail of dirty socks.

LEE. (*Finding it.*) Garlic! (*She shakes the garlic powder in his face.*)

BOB. (*Covering his face.*) I'm blind. I'm blind. What are you doing?

LEE. (*Still shaking.*) I'm sprinkling you to death with garlic powder.

BOB. I said sprinkle, not bury.

LEE. (*Still shaking.*) I wanted to make sure.

BOB. Will you stop! (*Snatching the shaker.*) You always use too much garlic.

LEE. Now, will you leave me alone.

BOB. Not only am I blind, but my eyes smell.

LEE. Serves you right. (*The buzzer sounds again, more insistently.* PAT *enters from the bedroom and crosses to, and presses the button by, the front door.*)

PAT. Are you going to let him in or not?

LEE. Who? (BOB *puts on his shoes, but not his socks.*)

PAT. Tracy with the paper. He buzzed ages ago.

LEE. I didn't notice.

PAT. Have you been cooking?

LEE. No, why?

PAT. There's an incredible smell of garlic.

BOB. It's my eyes.

LEE. We spilled some garlic powder.

PAT. Listen, do you mind if I stay in here and watch you fight, 'cos I've done about all there is to do in the bedroom?

BOB. Feel free, it's your apartment, but there isn't going to be anymore fighting.

PAT. Why not?

BOB. Because I drove here last night hoping that Lee and I might get back together. I have done my damndest to get us back together, but my damndest wasn't good enough. I do want to say that we did have some good times together. Actually we had three good times together, all of them after parties at the Ferguson's. But since I've arrived I've been (*Indicating the sofa, tub, ice-bucket, radio, garlic-powder, and* LEE *respectively.*) stretched, cramped, drenched, deafened, seasoned, and called a slob. I have a splitting headache, an empty stomach, and smelly eyes. I am now going to go downstairs, get some doughnuts, and drive home. You can stay 'here or move on, keep it a secret or publish it in the Daily News, it makes no difference to me, I shall be at home, in bed, in my pajamas. Goodbye. (*He turns and starts to the door, has an afterthought, and turns back.*) Still for old time's sake, I'd hate to think I was forgotten. So here's something to remember me by. (*He throws his socks, which he has been holding, down on the floor between them. Down center. He turns on his heel, crosses to the door, snatches it open and exits. In the doorway, he collides with* TRACY, *who is returning with the paper. Sections of the paper are scattered everywhere.* BOB *continues out,* TRACY, *faintly dazed, enters.*)

TRACY. I gather he left?

LEE. Yes, but you can tell he's been here. There are socks and newspapers all over the floor.

PAT. (*Brightly.*) Maybe he'll come back.

LEE. No.

PAT. Maybe he'll change his mind.

LEE. Well, if he does, he won't find me here. I'm leaving as soon as I've packed.

PAT. Where are you going?

LEE. I don't know. A hotel for tonight, then, I don't know. Maybe Oregon.

TRACY. Why Oregon?

LEE. Why not? (*Breaking, toward the bedroom, from the position she has held since the beginning of* BOB'S *speech.*) What's it matter? I'd better get dressed. (*Exits to the bedroom.*)

TRACY. Wow, what happened?

PAT. They didn't get back together.

TRACY. I know that. I mean before.

PAT. They had a terrible fight.

TRACY. What about?

PAT. You know, all the things married people fight about; vampires, pajamas, the Fergusons and garlic.

TRACY. What?

PAT. Well, I was in the bedroom. I didn't hear it all.

TRACY. Did she tell him what she told us, that she realized she wanted to go back?

PAT. I'm not sure. I don't think she had a chance.

TRACY. They might have got it together if we hadn't been here.

PAT. Why?

TRACY. Too many people in too small a space.

PAT. Your reasearch grant is pretty big, isn't it?

TRACY. It's okay, why?

PAT. You may be right about too many people. If we each paid a little more rent, we wouldn't need another roommmate. Could you afford a little more?

TRACY. Yeah, I guess so.

PAT. Of course, if we do that, we should really fix it up a bit more, make it comfortable.

TRACY. I suppose we could repaint it.

PAT. Yeah, and get some better bookcases. And get rid of this couch, I mean for a while we needed it, but we don't now and I've never really liked it. The room will look much better without the couch and that convertible ottoman. You'll love the way it looks.

TRACY. You mean empty?

PAT. No, not empty. We'll get two big armchairs and a coffee table.

TRACY. Anything else?

PAT. No, that's about it. Leave the bedroom as is for now, maybe a new spread. How does it sound?

TRACY. (*Completely aware.*) What if your mother arrives unexpectedly from out of town?

PAT. She wouldn't do that. She lives too far away.

TRACY. Where does she live?

PAT. Brooklyn.

TRACY. You know, I think we ought to leave.

PAT. Lee may need help with her luggage.

TRACY. She'd rather be left alone.

PAT. Where are we going to go?

TRACY. I dunno. Just out.

PAT. We can window shop, for furniture. (LEE *enters from the bedroom, dressed, and carrying some clothes which she packs into the suitcase.*)

LEE. I know I'm going to forget something, I always do.

PAT. (*Indicating.*) Like the socks.

LEE. I haven't forgotten the socks. I won't forget those socks, ever.

TRACY. You don't have to leave, you know.

PAT. There's not really any point after . . . what happened.

LEE. I know, but . . . I'd better leave.

TRACY. Well, listen we're gonna go.

LEE. Where are you going?

TRACY. Out.

PAT. Walking.

LEE. Oh.

TRACY. (*Indicating her costume.*) You're not going like that.

PAT. Why not?

TRACY. Because I don't go out with pregnant sailors, and I'm tired of talking to Shirley Temple, Scarlett O'Hara and Judy Garland.

PAT. I don't do Judy Garland.

LEE. Simon does a terrific Judy Garland.

PAT. (*Crossing to the bedroom.*) Well, Simon's gone back to bed, so can I wear some of your clothes?

TRACY. Wear your own.

PAT. Okay, but it won't really be me. (*Exits to bedroom.*)

LEE. You may be going to meet your new roommate.

TRACY. Looks that way.

LEE. Well, don't make my mistakes.

TRACY. Wasn't really your fault.

LEE. I didn't mean to say he was a slob. It's true, but I didn't mean to say it.

TRACY. He'll get over it.

LEE. Think so?

TRACY. Sure. May take a while, though.

LEE. I gather you and Pat are gonna stay on here?

TRACY. Yeah.

LEE. Well, at least you won't feel like your crowded rats, anymore.

TRACY. I guess, if two people are . . . together, then they're always a little crowded; I mean, whatever the size of their·place, you know. They just have to try and fit. (*Taking something out of* LEE's *hand, and re-arranging things in the suitcase.*) Like if you put this in first, your suitcase is gonna hold more.

LEE. That's Bob and me; a badly packed suitcase.

TRACY. Next time you see Bob . . .

LEE. (*Cutting off.*) I'm not going to see Bob.

TRACY. I know, but next time you see him, tell him the truth.

LEE. What is it?

TRACY. How you really feel. Tell him.

LEE. Did I tell *you* I had a great time last night?

TRACY. I'm glad.

LEE. Maybe I should've asked you out more often. We never did dance.

TRACY. And you didn't bring me the flowers or candy.

LEE. Well, you can't have everything. We did go walking.

TRACY. Yes. (PAT *enters from the bedroom, without a wig, wearing her own clothes. She wears glasses and a shirt and blouse and closely resembles* TRACY's *description in Act Two, Scene 1. That description may be al-*

tered to fit the actress, but the description and it's realiza-
tion should be very understated.)

PAT. Well, these are my clothes and this is my hair,
and you know who I look like?

LEE. Who?

PAT. Simon.

TRACY. You look fine.

LEE. You really do.

PAT. *(To* LEE.) Listen, when you get to wherever it
is, give us a call.

LEE. I will.

PAT. Are you sure you don't want us to help with
the luggage?

LEE. No, thanks.

PAT. *(Going to the front door.)* Keep in touch.

LEE. You know, you came out best of all, Pat?

PAT. How's that?

LEE. You got the one without a problem.

PAT. Oh, he has a problem.

LEE. What's that?

PAT. *(Smoothly.)* An inability to articulate the intimate.

TRACY. Oh, my God!

PAT. But I'm working on it.

TRACY. *(A touch uneasily.)* Listen, I just thought of
something. What if *my* mother arrives unexpectedly from
out of town? What'll I do?

PAT. Sleep in the tub. *(She pushes* TRACY *ahead of her
out of the front door, and follows him, closing it. They
are gone.* LEE *gathers from the room whatever she un-
packed in Act One, and packs it. She crosses to the telephone, picks it up and dials.)*

LEE. Hello, Miriam, Lee . . . Listen, I just called to
tell you I'm moving again and . . . What? . . . No, I
can't call back later. Miriam, can you fold your blankets?
. . . You can, then it isn't a real hangover . . . And I
don't care if you have a hangover, because I have a life
and it's not working. *(She hangs up. She looks around*

and then exits to the bedroom. She re-enters almost immediately with another armful of things to pack and her carry-all bag. At the same time she re-enters, BOB enters from the front door. He is still somewhat hungover and looks as if he's had some other, unknown shock. He carries a small bag of doughnuts. They come face to face, Down center, on either side of the socks. Pause. Then BOB bends over and picks up the socks. LEE tossing things onto the sofa. Very quickly.) I love you, I love you, I love you. That's what I meant to say this morning, but I didn't get a chance. Listen, in the last week I've learned a lot. I've learned you're a slob, I'm a rotten cook, and neither of us eats lamb-chops. We're two imperfect people, Bob. We fit.

BOB. They towed away my station wagon.

LEE. And you felt it too, didn't you? That's why you came back, isn't it? Isn't that why you came back? Why did you come back?

BOB. They towed away my station wagon. It's gone.

LEE. Maybe you forgot where you parked it?

BOB. No, I remember where I parked it, right in front of the fire-hydrant. It's gone.

LEE. We'll get it back. It only costs seventy-five dollars.

BOB. I don't have seventy-five dollars. I have two dollars and eleven cents and six jelly doughnuts.

LEE. Well, tomorrow you can cash a check and get it back. We'll take the train and have the Fergusons meet us.

BOB. I spent extra for white-wall tires and interior trim.

LEE. *(Finishing packing.)* Never mind. We'll get it back. Now, I think that's everything. You can carry the suitcase. *(He is still standing in his original position holding the bag and the socks.)* Bob! *(She snatches the socks from him and throws them down, and replaces them with the suitcase.)* Let's just go.

BOB. You're going with me?

LEE. Yes, of course.

BOB. Why?

LEE. My sewing machine's in the station wagon.

BOB. By the way . . . before we go.

LEE. Yes?

BOB. When you drew straws to see who would sleep with whom. Who did sleep with whom?

LEE. I'm not going to tell you.

BOB. Of course, you are.

LEE. No, I'm not. It's a secret.

BOB. We said we'd never have secrets. Now, tell me. Who slept with whom?

LEE. What's it matter? Sleeping with people is easy; living with them is hard.

BOB. But I want to know.

LEE. All right. I'll tell you. (*The phone rings.* BOB, *who is nearest to it, picks it up and answers.*)

BOB. (*Irritated.*) Hello . . . What? . . . Listen, it's Sunday morning. . . . Nobody needs a strange roommate on Sunday morning . . . (*Looking at* LEE.) No, I just found a new roommate; a permanent one . . . (*At that,* LEE *crosses over to him, picking up Bernice on the way.*) I don't care if it's an emergency; we're overcrowded now . . . Three exotic dancers who've lost your luggage? Well, maybe we could make accommodations for you if . . . (*But* LEE *has taken the receiver from him and hung up.*)

CURTAIN

PROPERTY LIST

Act One:

TRACY:
  2 suitcases
  overnight case
  small television set
  towel
  shaving kit

LEE:
  handbag, containing:
    notepaper
    pencil
    nail file
  large carry-all bag, containing:
    small skillet
    clock
    can of disinfectant spray
    stuffed toy pig
    tape measure

PAT:
  large lollipop
  small grocery sack, containing:
    2 cans of Coca-Cola
    jar of peanut butter

Preset:
  bar of soap (kitchen counter)
  newspaper (kitchen counter)
  brown garbage bag (under kitchen counter)

Act Two, Scene One:

TRACY:
  textbook
  index cards
  ballpoint pen

PAT:
  cigarette

LEE:
  Department store shopping bag (Macy's), containing:
    throw pillow
    three bright mugs
    small potted plant
    plastic garbage pail
  ten dollar bill in handbag

Preset:
  radio (on bookcase)
  brown garbage bag (under kitchen counter)
  pair of socks (on the floor beside the ottoman)
  drinking glasses (on kitchen shelves)
  bottle of Scotch or pre-mixed cocktail (kitchen shelves)
  ice cubes (refrigerator, already out of tray)
  ashtray (table)

Act Two, Scene Two:

BOB:
  cigarettes
  lighter or matches

Preset:
  1 empty wine bottle (table)
  1 nearly full wine bottle (table)
  1 dinner plate, empty (table)
  1 dinner plate with lamb chops and artichokes (table, food
    need not be practical)
  2 wine glasses (table)
  appropriate flatware (table)
  pepper and salt (table)
  2 small bowls or plates, empty (table)
  ashtray (table)
  candle in candleholder (table)
  2 drinking glasses (kitchen shelves)
  bottle of Gin (kitchen shelves)
  bottle of Vermouth (kitchen shelves)
  ice bucket with cubes (kitchen counter)

Act Three:

LEE:
   2 piles of folded clothes
   small hairdryer
   carry-all bag
   handbag

BOB:
   small doughnut bag

PAT:
   coffee pot

TRACY:
   New York Sunday Times (put together to fall apart easily)

Preset:
   table as in Act Two, Scene Two
   ice bucket full of water (table)
   feather boa (couch)
   rumpled blanket (couch)
   pillow (couch)
   2 drinking glasses (kitchen shelves)
   pitcher with orange juice (refrigerator)
   towel (towel rack)
   3 coffee mugs (kitchen counter)
   carton of milk (refrigerator)
   damp blanket (inside tub)
   suitcase (under bookcase or somewhere like that)
   bottle or can of garlic (kitchen shelves)
   toy stuffed pig (bookcase)

SET AND SET DRESSING

Act One:

    bare kitchen table
2 plain, unmatched kitchen chairs
window either bare or covered with a broken Venetian blind
Indian cloth curtain over the bedroom entrance
2 cracked cups, a plate and a can of beans on the kitchen
    shelves
1 old pot on the stove
1 large, convertible ottoman (need not be practical)

Act Two, Scene One and the rest of the play:

    table, chairs, and ottoman as before
if possible, use two identical sets of plain, unmatched kitchen
    chairs, and for Act Two and Three use a set that have
    been painted a bright colour to match each other
cheerful curtains over the window
tablecloth of the same fabric
bookcase and books
the toy, stuffed pig should remain in the bookcase until picked
    up at the end of Act Three
ordinary attractive couch
towel rack put up near tub, with attractive towels on it
stacks of clean plates, glasses etc., on kitchen shelves
selection of canned and packaged food on kitchen shelves
assortment of spices on kitchen shelves
Lee's suitcase under bookcase, or somewhere suitable
Beaded curtain over or replacing Indian cloth curtain
a table lamp somewhere
possible additions:
    trunk used both as occasional table and seat
    pictures on the walls
the improvement in the apartment should be pleasant and
    noticeable, but not spectacular

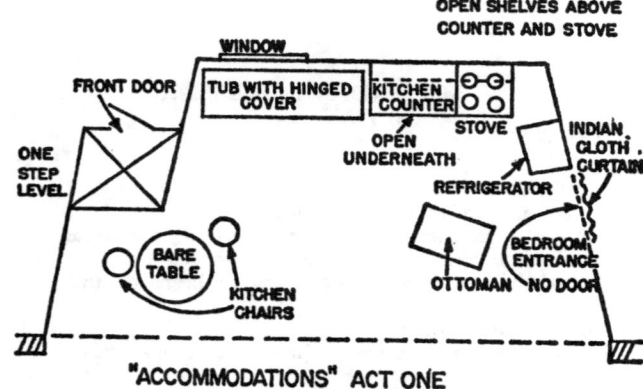

OPEN SHELVES ABOVE
COUNTER AND STOVE

WINDOW

FRONT DOOR

TUB WITH HINGED
COVER

KITCHEN
COUNTER

STOVE

OPEN
UNDERNEATH

INDIAN
CLOTH
CURTAIN

ONE
STEP
LEVEL

REFRIGERATOR

BARE
TABLE

KITCHEN
CHAIRS

BEDROOM
ENTRANCE
NO DOOR

OTTOMAN

"ACCOMMODATIONS" ACT ONE

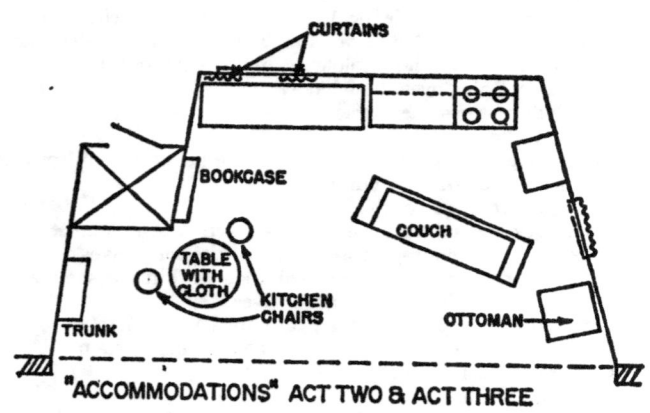

CURTAINS

BOOKCASE

COUCH

TABLE
WITH
CLOTH

KITCHEN
CHAIRS

OTTOMAN

TRUNK

"ACCOMMODATIONS" ACT TWO & ACT THREE

72

Also By

Nick Hall

BESIDE YOURSELF

BROKEN UP

DEAD WRONG

EAT YOUR HEART OUT

GOING APE

MARRIAGE IS MURDER

PASTICHE

SAMUELFRENCH.COM

OTHER TITLES AVAILABLE FROM SAMUEL FRENCH

PERFECT WEDDING
Robin Hawdon

Comedy / 2m, 4f / Interior
A man wakes up in the bridal suite on his wedding morning to find an extremely attractive naked girl in bed beside him. In the depths of a stag night hangover, he can't even remember meeting her. Before he can get her out, his bride to be arrives to dress for the wedding. In the ensuing panic, the girl is locked in the bathroom. The best man is persuaded to claim her, but he gets confused and introduces the chamber maid to the bride as his date. The crisis escalates to nuclear levels by the time the mother of the bride and the best man's actual girlfriend arrive. This rare combination of riotous farce and touching love story has provoked waves of laughter across Europe and America.

"Laughs abound."
– *Wisconsin Advocate*

"The full house audience roared with delight."
– *Green Bay Gazette*

OTHER TITLES AVAILABLE FROM SAMUEL FRENCH

THE DECORATOR
Donald Churchill

Comedy / 1m, 2f / Interior

Marcia returns to her flat to find it has not been painted as she arranged. A part time painter who is filling in for an ill colleague is just beginning the work when the wife of the man with whom Marcia is having an affair arrives to tell all to Marcia's husband. Marcia hires the painter a part time actor to impersonate her husband at the confrontation. Hilarity is piled upon hilarity as the painter, who takes his acting very seriously, portrays the absent husband. The wronged wife decides that the best revenge is to sleep with Marcia's husband, an ecstatic experience for them both. When Marcia learns that the painter/actor has slept with her rival, she demands the opportunity to show him what really good sex is.

"Irresistible."
– *London Daily Telegraph*

"This play will leave you rolling in the aisles....
I all but fell from my seat laughing."
– *London Star*

TAKE HER, SHE'S MINE

Phoebe and Henry Ephron

Comedy / 11m, 6f / Various Sets

Art Carney and Phyllis Thaxter played the Broadway roles of parents of two typical American girls enroute to college. The story is based on the wild and wooly experiences the authors had with their daughters, Nora Ephron and Delia Ephron, themselves now well known writers. The phases of a girl's life are cause for enjoyment except to fearful fathers. Through the first two years, the authors tell us, college girls are frightfully sophisticated about all departments of human life. Then they pass into the "liberal" period of causes and humanitarianism, and some into the intellectual lethargy of beatniksville. Finally, they start to think seriously of their lives as grown ups. It's an experience in growing up, as much for the parents as for the girls.

"A warming comedy. A delightful play about parents vs kids. It's loaded with laughs. It's going to be a smash hit."
– *New York Mirror*

THREE YEARS FROM "THIRTY"
Mike O'Malley

Comic Drama / 4m, 3f / Unit set

This funny, poignant story of a group of 27-year-olds who have known each other since college sold out during its limited run at New York City's Sanford Meisner Theater. Jessica Titus, a frustrated actress living in Boston, has become distraught over local job opportunities and she is feeling trapped in her long standing relationship with her boyfriend Tom. She suddenly decides to pursue her dreams in New York City. Unbeknownst to her, Tom plans to propose on the evening she has chosen to leave him. The ensuing conflict ripples through their lives and the lives of their roommates and friends, leaving all of them to reconsider their careers, the paths of their souls and the questions, demands and definition of commitment.